W9-AOK-059

This book is dedicated to Gina, Ace, and Ava. They are my everything and the driving, everlasting force of love behind *Made For Me*. Much like my family, this book is my dream come true. -Z.B.

Published by Familius LLC.
1254 Commerce Way, Sanger, CA 93657.
www.familius.com

Library of Congress Cataloging-in-Publication Data
2017956664
ISBN 9781945547690
eISBN 9781641700054

Book and jacket design by David Miles

Printed in China

10 9 8 7 6 5 4 3 2

First Edition

ZACK BUSH

ILLUSTRATIONS BY

GREGORIO DE LAURETIS

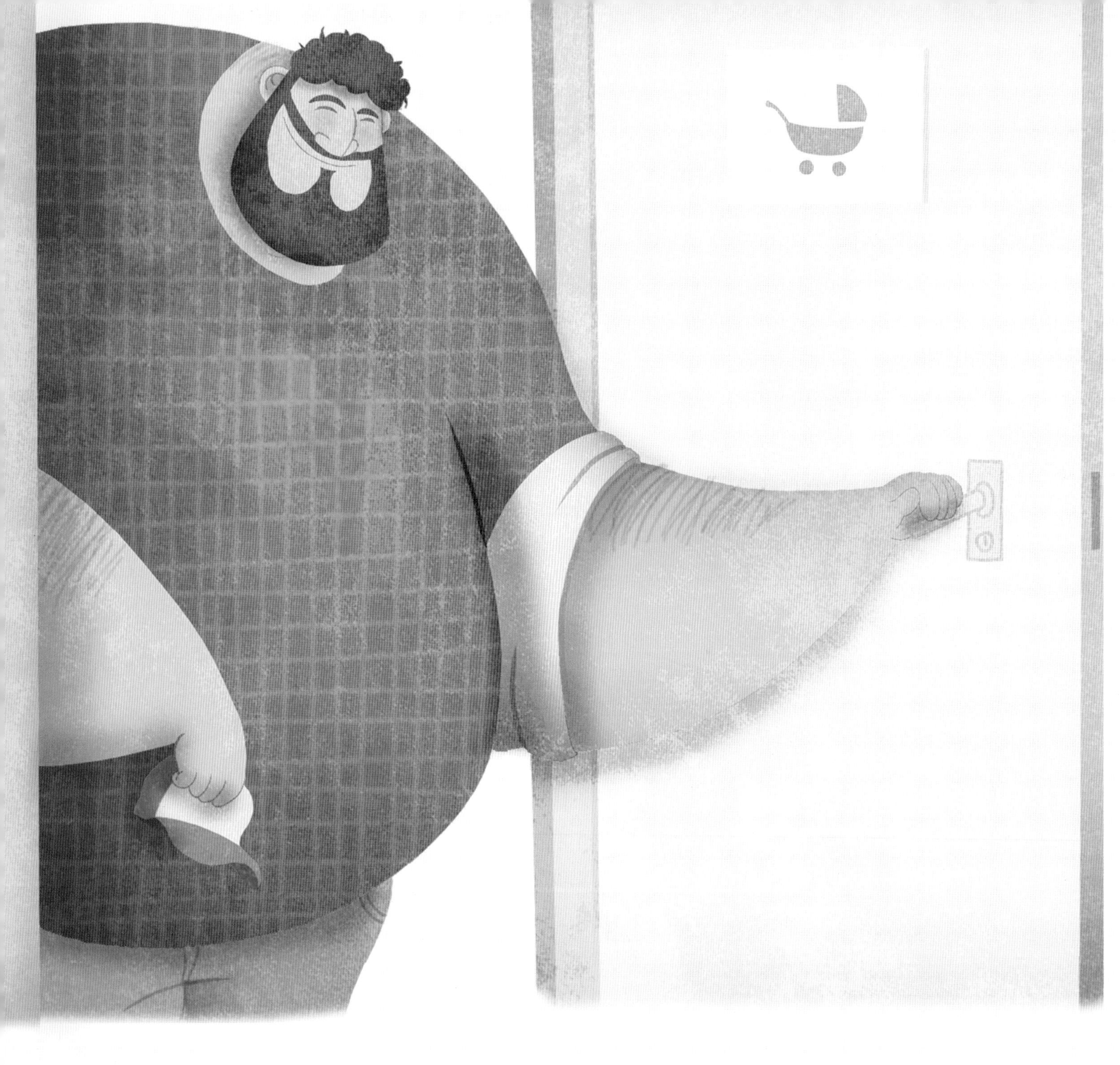

On the day you were born, I beamed with pride.
My eyes filled with tears. I joyfully cried.

From the moment I saw you and called out your name,
the world as I knew it was never the same.

I held you so gently, up close to my chest.
Nestled so cozy—this day was the best!

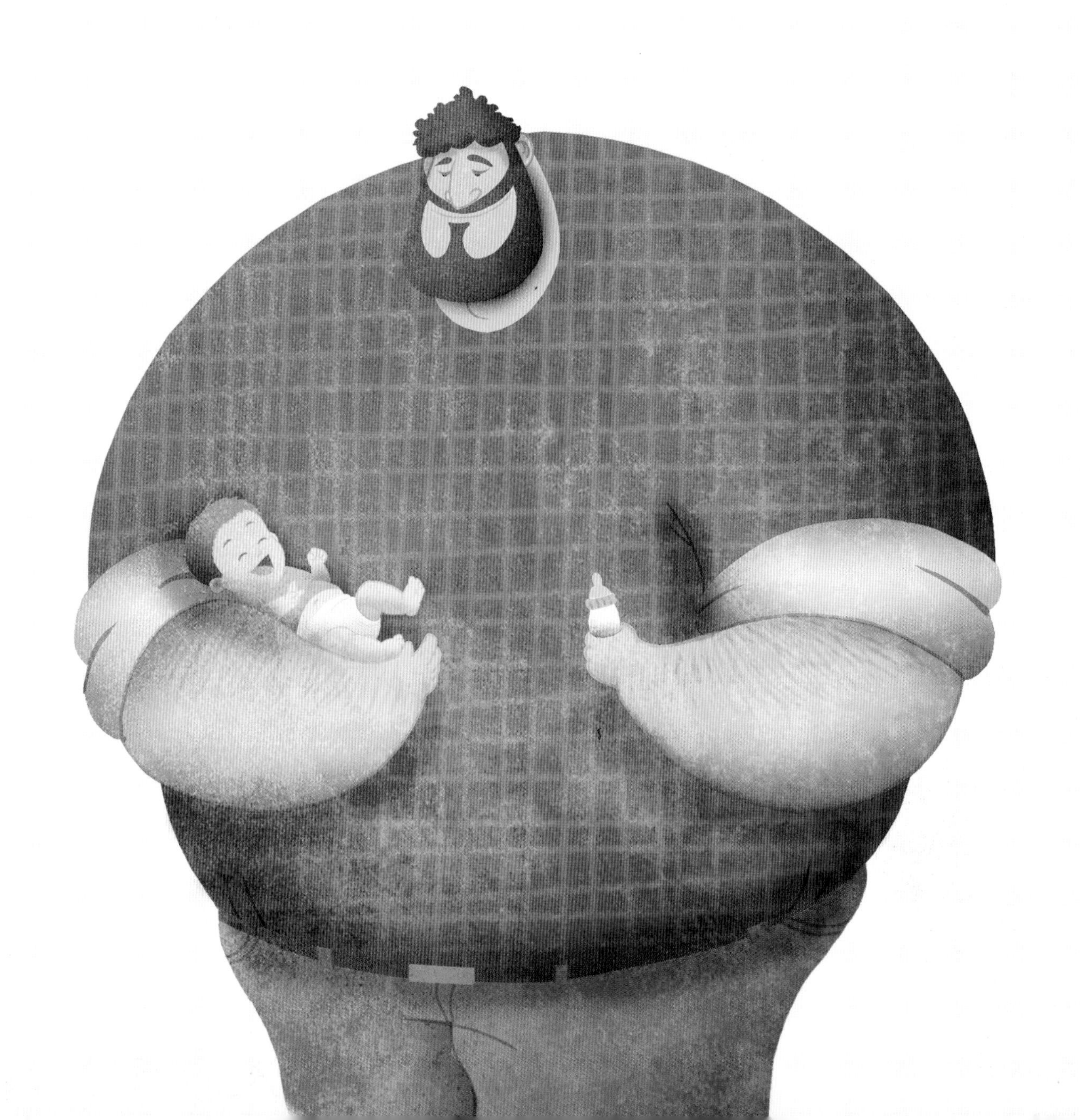

My new role in life
had just now begun.
You're life's greatest
treasure, my dear little one.

Of all the children that ever could be,
you are the one made just for me.

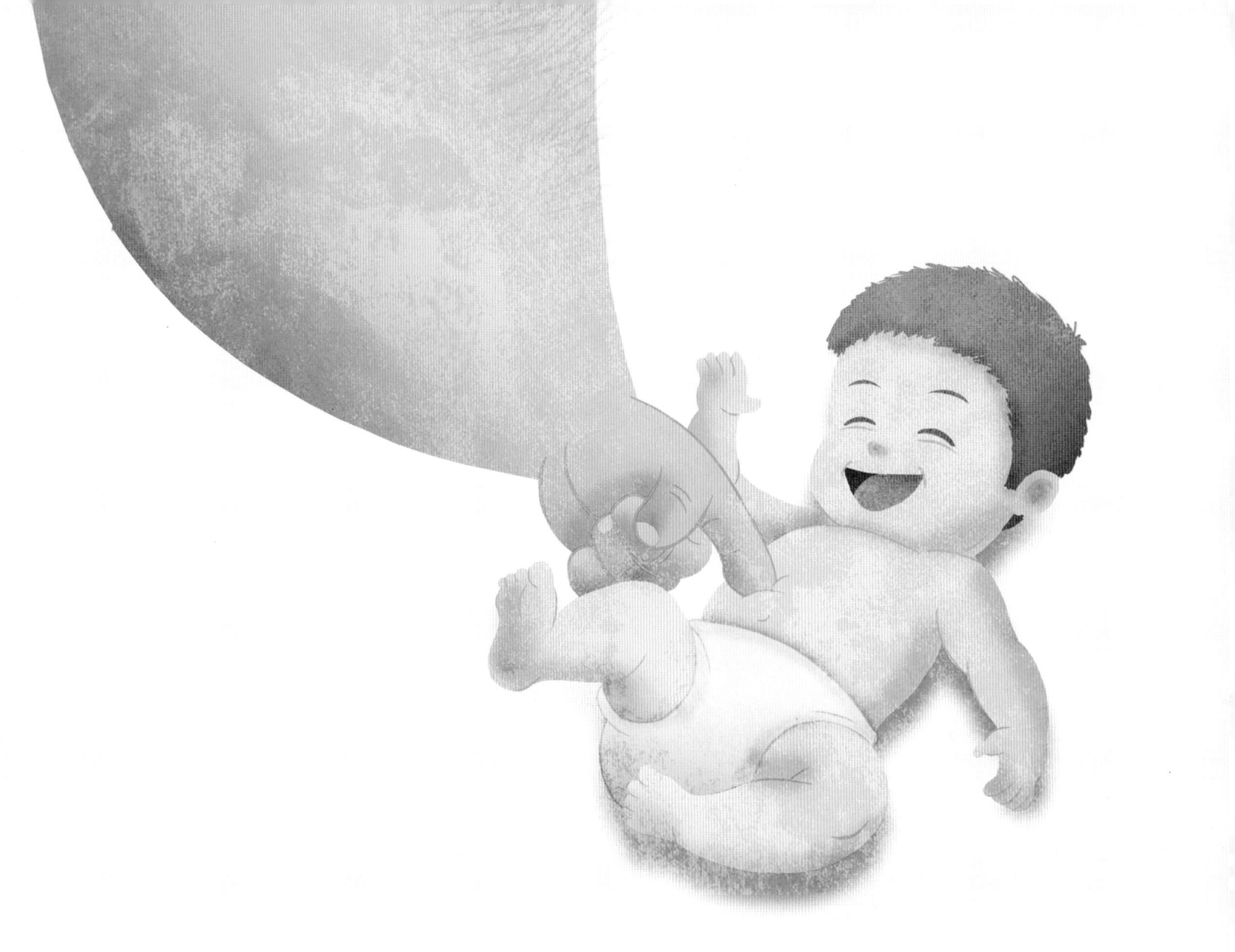

Awed and amazed, this was only the start.
From your hands to your feet, I loved every part!

Your mouth, your ears, and even your nose,
your chubby cheeks and your wiggly toes.

I'll never forget your sweet little grin.
Your soft, tiny hands. Your smooth, rounded chin.

I cherished each moment you looked in my eyes.
I stood by your side, through laughter and cries.

Of all the children that ever could be,
you are the one made just for me.

You crawled through the house and began to explore.
You peeked behind curtains and in every drawer.

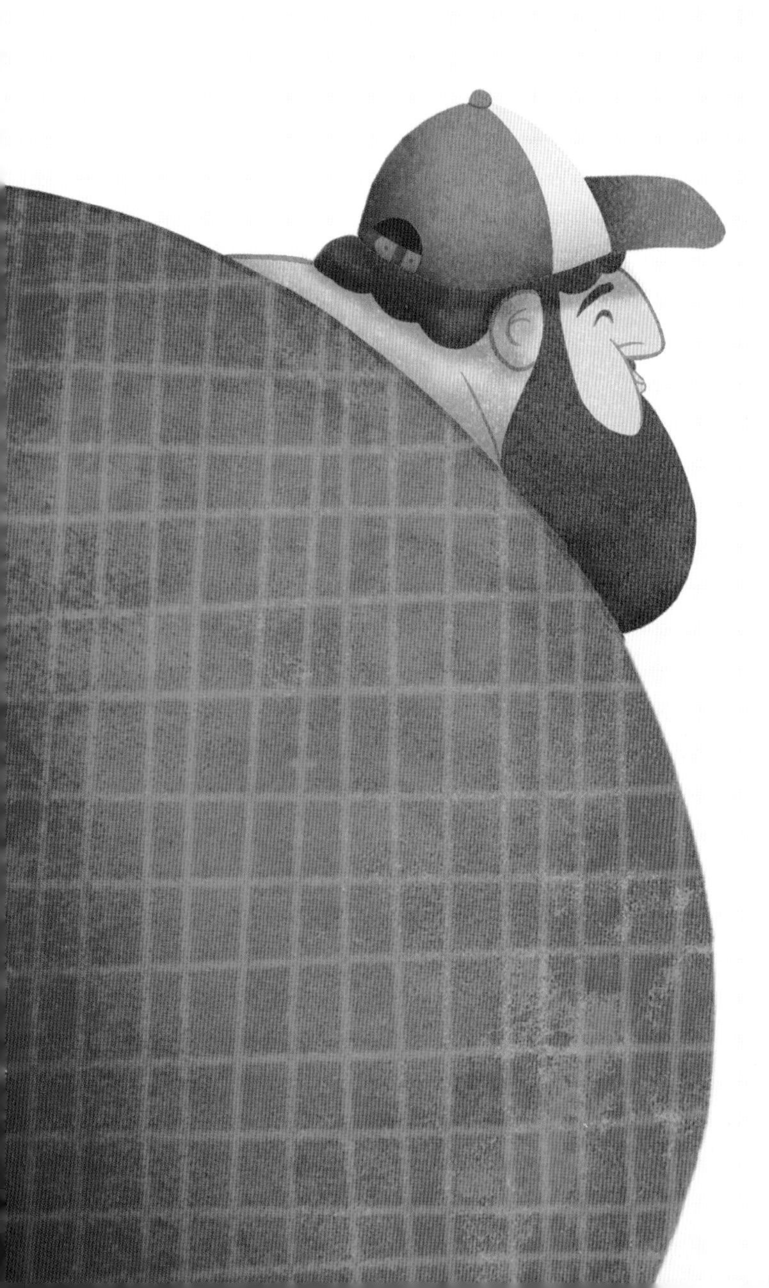

With amazement and wonder, and never too serious,
you'd babble and giggle—always so curious!

With comfort I calmed you and came to your aid—
always together so you weren't afraid.

Each morning, I'd wake so excited for you
to discover the world and try something new.

Of all the children that ever could be,
you are the one made just for me.

You stood, then fell, but learned how to walk.
You said "Mama" and "Dada" and started to talk.

You laughed with delight as you slid at the park
and clapped the first time you heard a dog bark.

You loved to bang pots and put on a show.
You, my sweet child, were beginning to grow.

I rocked you to sleep in a cradle so tight.
I melted when you first kissed ME goodnight.

Of all the children that ever could be,
you are the one made just for me.

A trip to the beach set the wheels in motion.
You built a sandcastle, took a dip in the ocean.

I saved the first curl that was snipped from your head.
I watched as you climbed into your new big bed!

You played in the park. Swung a bat. Tossed a ball,
Spent summers poolside. Raked leaves in the fall.

You rolled in the grass. Stared at clouds up above.
I watched you being you, and it's you that I love.

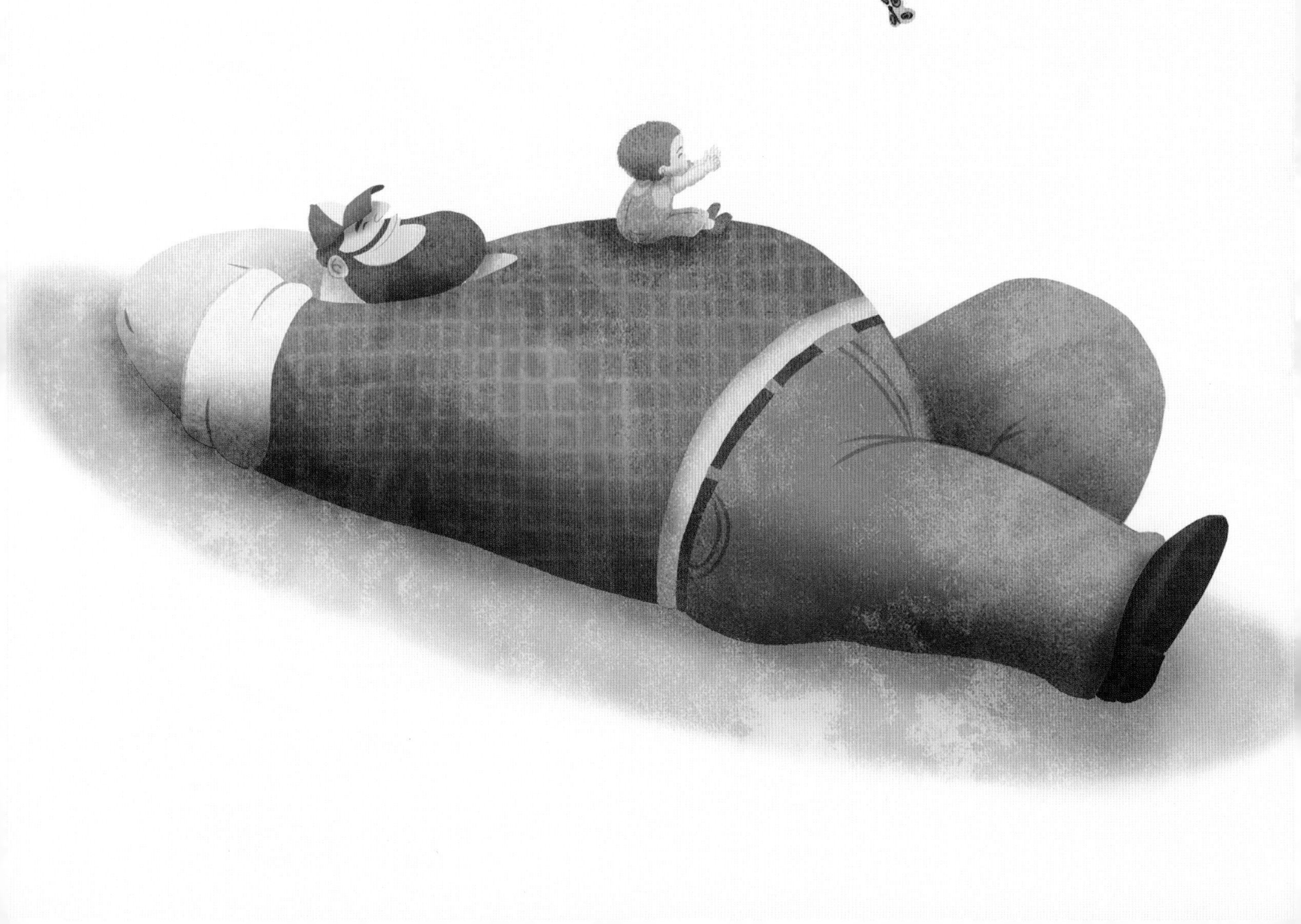

Of all the children that ever could be,
you are the one made just for me.

From the day you were born, so cute and so clever,
you're one-of- a-kind, and I'll love you forever!

It's now time to sleep.
Rest your beautiful eyes.
Soon the dark night will
turn to blue skies.

Tucked in tight, it's my heart where you'll stay.
Tomorrow I'll love you even more than today.

Of all the children that ever could be,
you are the one made just for me.